The Afternoon of a Writer

Peter Handke

THE AFTERNOON

OF A WRITER

Translated by Ralph Manheim

Farrar Straus Giroux

New York

Fic

Originally published in German under the title Nachmittag eines
Schriftstellers, *copyright © 1987 by Residenz Verlag, Salzburg und Wien*
Published simultaneously in Canada by Collins Publishers, Toronto
Printed in the United States of America
Designed by Cynthia Krupat
First edition, 1989

Library of Congress Cataloging-in-Publication Data
Handke, Peter.
[Nachmittag eines Schriftstellers. English]
The afternoon of a writer / Peter Handke;
translated by Ralph Manheim.—1st ed.
Translation of: Nachmittag eines Schriftstellers.
I. Title.
PT2668.A5N3413   1989   833'.914—dc20   89-7741

R00711 20140

for F. Scott Fitzgerald

The Afternoon of a Writer

EVER SINCE the time when he lived for almost a year with the thought that he had lost contact with language, every sentence he managed to write, and which in addition left him feeling that it might be possible to go on, had been an event. Every word, not spoken but written, that led to others, filled his lungs with air and renewed his tie with the world. A successful notation of this kind began the day for him; after that, or at least so he thought, nothing could happen to him until the following morning.

But perhaps this fear of coming to a standstill, of not being able to go on, of having to break off forever, had been with him all his life, in connection not only with writing but with all his other under-

3]

takings: loving, studying, participating—everything, in short, that called for perseverance. Perhaps his professional problem was a parable of his existence, for it clearly exemplified his situation. In other words, not "I as writer" but "the writer as I." And indeed it was only since the period when he feared that he had strayed beyond the frontiers of language and would never find his way home and the ensuing period of having to begin again day after day and with no assurance of success that he, whose guiding thought for more than half a lifetime had been the thought of writing, had seriously regarded himself as a writer—a word which up until then he had used only ironically or sheepishly.

And now, thanks to a few lines that had clarified a state of affairs to his satisfaction and given it new life, he had the impression that the day had gone well, and stood up from his desk with the feeling that it was all right for the day to be over. He didn't know what time it was. In his mind, it was only a moment ago that the midday bells of the chapel of the old people's home at the foot of the little hill had suddenly started tinkling as though someone had died, yet hours must have passed since then, for the light in the room was now an afternoon light.

He took the shimmer of sunlight on the carpet as a
sign that his work had measured out the right
amount of time. He raised both arms and bowed to
the sheet of paper in his typewriter. At the same
time he told himself, as he had so often, that he
must not lose himself in his work the next day, but
on the contrary use it to open up his senses: instead
of taking his mind off his work, the shadow of a bird
darting across the wall should accompany and clarify his writing, and so should the barking of a dog,
the whining of a chain saw, the grinding of trucks
shifting gears, the constant hammering, the inces-
sant whistle blowing and shouts of command from
the schoolyards and drill grounds down in the plain.
And then it occurred to him, as it had for a number
of days, that in his last hour at his desk the only
sounds to have reached him from the city were police
and ambulance sirens and that he had not once, as
he had earlier in the day, looked up from his paper
and turned toward the window to concentrate on the
sight of a tree trunk in the garden, or the cat eyeing
him from the outer window ledge, or the planes in
the sky, landing from left to right and taking off
from right to left. At first he was unable to focus on
anything in the distance and saw even the pattern
of the carpet as a blur; in his ears he heard a buzzing

as though his typewriter were an electric one—which was not the case.

The writer's workroom—his "den"—was on the second floor. Bemused, carrying his empty teacup, he went downstairs and saw by the kitchen clock that the day was almost over. It was early December and the edges of various objects glowed as they do at the onset at twilight. At the same time, the airy space outside and the interior of the curtainless house seemed joined in an undivided brightness. No snow had yet fallen that year. But that morning the birds had cheeped in a certain way—in a monotone suggestive of speech—that heralded snow. Standing in the light, which little by little restored his senses, the writer felt impelled to go out. On those days when he did not leave the house until it was beginning to get dark, he felt that he had missed something. Strange that someone in his profession had always felt most at home out of doors.

In the entrance, he bent down and picked up the mail which the postman had pushed through the slot in the door. The one thing in the thick pile that he wanted to read was a picture postcard. There were advertising circulars, political fliers, free sam-

[6

ples, and invitations to art galleries or so-called town meetings—but more than half the pile consisted of the familiar gray envelopes, all addressed in the hand of the same unknown individual, who for more than ten years had been sending him almost daily at least a dozen such letters from some remote foreign country. Long ago the writer, for no other reason than because at first glance he had mistaken the stranger's handwriting for his own, had replied briefly to the first letter. Since then, the sender had taken the tone of a childhood friend or of an old garden-fence neighbor. The envelopes always contained fragmentary messages, as a rule no more than one sentence, about the stranger's family life, his wife and children, such as "Today a registered letter from my wife," or "She has forbidden me to see them." Puzzling remarks such as "Better to die than to buy a plane ticket against my will," or "She can't deny that I weeded the garden yesterday"; or mere outcries on the order of "I wish I could finally be happy," or "I, too, am entitled to a new life"—as if the addressee had known the sender's whole story for ages. In the first years the writer had carefully read every one of the incoherent sentences and even each of the disjointed words. But as time went on, these scraps of paper had begun to depress him, especially on the not unusual days when they were his only mail. On those days he wished his correspondent could see the fury with which he clamped the lid of the garbage pail down on the stack of unopened envelopes. From time to time, when an infrequent sense of duty led him to open one of the envelopes, he was almost comforted to see that the news appeared to be always the same. True, the letters were cries for help, entreaties, but even if no one heard them, they seemed capable of going on for a lifetime. And this, apart from laziness, was why the writer did not have the letters returned to sender—as he often felt tempted to do at the sight of the daily rectangular airmail letters, unaccompanied by so much as a sign of life from anyone else. This time he relegated the whole pile to the wastepaper basket, as he had yesterday, depositing each envelope separately, as if that were a sort of acknowledgment. The picture postcard—from a one-time friend now in America, who was wandering about that continent in a state of confusion—he slipped into his coat pocket to read when he went out.

He showered, changed his clothes, and put on shoes of a type equally well adapted to sidewalks, escalators, and rough country. He let the cat into the house and set out dishes of meat and milk. The cold seemed to have accumulated in the cat's fur, and the writer thought he detected a suggestion of snow crystals on the tips of its hairs. But the body underneath warmed his hands, which had grown cold with the hours of writing.

Eager though he was to go out, he hesitated as usual. He opened the doors to all the rooms on the ground floor, letting the light from different directions fuse. The house seemed uninhabited. He had the impression that, dissatisfied with being only worked in and slept in, it would have liked to be lived in as well. Of that the writer had probably been incapable from the start, as of any family life. He found window seats, dining tables, and pianos upsetting; stereo loudspeakers, chessboards and flower vases, even organized bookshelves repelled him—his books tended to pile up on the floor and windowsills. It was only at night, sitting somewhere in the dark, looking out into the rooms, which to his taste were sufficiently illuminated by the city lights and their reflection in the sky, that he almost had a sense of being at home. At last he had no need to ponder and plan, but just sat there quietly in the silence, at the most remembering; these were the hours when he was happiest to be in the house, and he always prolonged them until, imperceptibly, his musings merged into equally peaceful dreams. In the daytime, however, especially just after work, he soon found the silence oppressive. Then the splashing of the dishwasher in the kitchen or the hum of the dryer in the bathroom—if possible, both at once—came as a relief. Before even getting up from his desk, he needed the sounds of the outside world. Once, after months of writing in an almost sound-proof room in a high-rise building, close to the sky as it were, he had moved, in order to go on working, to a street-level room on a noisy traffic artery, and later, in the present house, though the construction noises next door had disturbed him at first, he had soon got used to hearing the din of the jackhammers and bulldozers every morning, very much as in the beginning he had played rock music to ease himself into work. From time to time, he would take his eyes off his paper, look out at the workers, and try to establish a harmony between what he was doing and their unhurried one-thing-after-another. He often needed a confrontation of this kind, which nature—the trees, the grass, the Virginia creeper twined around his window—could not in the long run provide. Be that as it may, a fly in the room disturbed him a lot, more than a pile driver outside.

On his way to the garden gate, the writer suddenly turned around. He rushed into the house and up to his study and substituted one word for another. It was only then that he smelled the sweat in the room and saw the mist on the windowpanes.

ALL AT ONCE, he was in less of a hurry. All at
once, because of this one word, the whole empty
house seemed warm and hospitable. On the threshold he turned back toward the desk, which for a
moment struck him as a place of righteousness or
of becoming righteous: "That is definitely how it
should be!" Down below, he installed himself in the
entrance—which was glassed in on the garden
side—sewed on some buttons, and cleaned several
pairs of summer shoes. While engaged in this ac-
tivity, he thought of the great poet who was said to
look "noble even when cutting his fingernails," and
doubted whether anyone could say that of him. Out
in the garden, a bird slipped Tom Thumb-like into
the conical yew tree and didn't come out again. The

droning of the single-engine planes overhead reminded him of Alaska, and the whistle of the trains
looping around the city also came from a distant
land rich in water. For a moment, the rumbling of
wheels in a switchyard on the horizon was clearly
audible; at the exact same moment, a dog scratched
itself at the foot of the stairs and the fridge hummed
in the pantry. For the second time that day, the
writer watered the plants in the entrance, which, in
conjunction with the glass wall, gave it the look of
a greenhouse, fed the cat again, and finally, polished
all the door handles. He felt an urge to write a letter,
no matter to whom, but not here in the house—
later, somewhere in town.

Once—during the time when he thought he was
losing contact with language—he had vowed never
again to lock a door behind him. This occurred to
him while he was double locking the door, as he did
every day when leaving the house. To make up
for his lapse, he resolved, he would leave the door
unlocked when he came home that night; had
he not, even without such an undertaking, found
the door not only unlocked but wide open some
mornings?

13]

On the clay of the garden path he walked in his own footprints, the consequence of his daily pacing, often for hours, before starting to work. Now they were frozen; a dense interlocking pattern was stamped into the ground the whole length of the garden, as though an army had come marching in, prepared for hand-to-hand combat, or as though a special police unit had come to arrest a dangerous public enemy. The writer recalled a comic film in which the hero plods back and forth outside a building for so long that his plodding carves out a ditch from which only his hat emerges.

Despite the wintry weather, there were still flowers here and there. Precisely because they were small and scattered, the catchfly, daisies, buttercups, and dead nettles enlivened the undulating landscape. A few bird-pecked apples were left in the crown of the one tree; their flesh was no doubt frozen glass-hard. The last leaves, weighed down by hoarfrost, fell to the ground one by one, almost vertically, with a crackling sound. The hazel catkins were colorless and seemed doubled-up with the cold. The bellflower by the picket fence was a frosty blue.

Next to the garden there was a small park which, as often happened at the end of the working day, looked to the writer like a primeval forest, rich in underbrush and creepers. Once he turned around to face the house, with the feeling that he had stepped out of a shadow. The sky was light gray, crisscrossed by long bands of a darker gray which left an impression of spaciousness and height. There was no wind, but the air was so cold that he felt it grazing his forehead and throat. At a fork in the road, he stopped. Which way should he go? In town there would be Christmas crowds; on the outskirts he would be alone. Ordinarily, in times of idleness, he would stroll into town. But when concentrating on his work, he usually went to the outskirts—out into the wilderness; thus far, he had adhered to this rule. But did he actually have any rules? Weren't the few that he had tried to impose on himself constantly giving way to something else—a mood, an accident, a sudden inspiration—that seemed to indicate the better choice? True, his life had been oriented for almost twenty years toward his literary goal; but reliable ways and means were still unknown to him. Everything about him was still as temporary as it had been in the child, as later in the

15]

schoolboy, and still later in the novice writer. Temporarily he was living, the same novice as before, in this unremarkable European city, although, so it seemed to him, he had begun to age here; he had returned, but only for the time being, from abroad to his own country, prepared to pick up and leave again at any moment and, as he saw it, even his life as a writer, close as it came to his dream, was also "for the time being"—the definitive had always repelled him. "All is flux," "You cannot step twice into the same river," or, in the original wording of the famous maxim: "You may step into the same river, but other and still other waters will flow past you." Through the years he had repeated Heraclitus' words to himself over and over again, very much as believers recite the "Our Father."

The writer stopped at the crossroads longer than usual. Perhaps because his profession did not impose a hard-and-fast schedule, he seemed to need an idea to carry him through the most trifling daily movements; the idea that came to him now was to combine the periphery with the center by crossing the inner city on his way to the outskirts. Hadn't he, while still at his desk, felt the need to be among people? And hadn't he time and again neglected his vow to cross the river at least once a day and explore newer districts of the city? Now that he had a plan, he was glad to be on the move.

It was quite a while before he saw anyone on his way downhill through the wooded park. Alone with nature after so many hours in his room, he felt free, buoyed by a childlike feeling. At last he had stopped mulling over the morning's sentences. Ignoring the bright-colored bird chart and the instructive BEECH and MAPLE signs on the corresponding tree trunks, he had eyes only for the light smoothness of the one tree and the roughness of the other. At the sight of a dozen sparrows sitting motionless, puffed up against the cold, in a stunted oak tree that had not yet lost all its leaves, he found himself believing in the legend of the saint who had preached to these little birds; and indeed the sparrows, without stirring from the spot, jerked their heads as though in anticipation of his first word. Whereupon he said something or other and the birds in the tree listened.

The road was yellow with fallen larch needles. Though ankle-deep at some bends in the road, they were piled so loosely that they dispersed under his footsteps, and the resulting streaks on the asphalt suggested meanders. As the silence around him deepened during his last hours in the house, he had been overwhelmed by the thought that the world outside had ceased to exist and that he in his room was the sole survivor. Consequently, he was vastly relieved to see a real, healthy-looking human being, a street sweeper who, having finished his day's work, stepped out of his toolshed in his street clothes, elaborately wiping his thick glasses with an enormous handkerchief. As they wished each other a good evening, it occurred to the writer that these were the first words he had exchanged that day; thus far, he had only listened in silence to the early-morning news, talked to the cat, and, seated at his desk, spoken a line or two aloud. As a result, he now had to clear his throat to prepare his voice for the customary man-to-man tone. Even if the nearsighted street sweeper couldn't quite see him, how comforting, after supposing that the world had come to an end, to encounter these two living, energetic eyes. He had the feeling that only the colors of those eyes could understand him, just as, reflected in their eyes, he was able to understand the faces of the passersby—who were becoming more and more frequent as he approached the city.

Although his house was on the hilltop, with windows opening out in all directions, he hadn't really looked into the distance that day. A distant view came to him only as his descent brought him among people. (At home he avoided the roof terrace for which visitors envied him, because the panorama made him feel too remote; he used it only to hang washing.) Now, in the mountains out of which the river burst, he saw a glassy snow field; and on the other side, at the edge of the plain, where the outer suburbs of the city were situated, a curved moraine that might have been sketched in with charcoal. It seemed to him that he might reach out and touch the moss and lichen under the snow, the brook cutting across the moraine, and on its banks outcroppings of ice, which made a clicking sound as the water rushed through. Beyond the housing developments on the periphery, he could see a row of smaller buildings, which, as he continued to look at them, moved through the countryside. He made out the Autobahn with its inaudible trucks, and for a moment he felt a vibration in his arms, as if he were driving one of them. Near the smokestacks of the industrial zone, in a strip of no-man's-land overgrown with bushes, a red light flared, and the dark container behind it turned out to be a stopped train, which, when the signals changed, set itself, at first almost imperceptibly, in motion, and grew larger as it approached. It would soon be pulling into the station, and most of the passengers had already put on their coats. A child's hand looked for a grown-up's hand. The travelers who were going farther stretched out their legs. The waiter in the almost empty dining car, who had been on duty since early morning, stepped out into the corridor, cranked down the window, and cooled his face in the breeze, while the dishwasher, an elderly meridional, sat in his cubbyhole, smoking and staring impassively into space. Along with these distant sights ("Distance, my thing") the writer saw, above the roofs of the inner city, above the dome of a church, standing out against the sky, a stone statue holding an iron palm branch, surrounded by secondary figures as though executing a round dance.

At the bottom of the hill the writer descended a stairway bordered by centuries-old urban houses. Here and there in the upper section, terraced gardens leapt like a row of drawbridges against the railing of the stairs. Farther down, close to the rocky slope, lights were on in all the rooms, as they had probably been all day. From each stair landing, one could look into a lower story of one of the houses. A table lamp cast a circle of light on a few open books, which the man sitting motionless at the table seemed to be staring at rather than reading. A woman was standing there in her coat and hat, still carrying a heavy shopping bag, as though she had just come in. A white-haired man with suspenders and rolled-up shirt sleeves walked slowly across the room with a coffeepot, followed a few steps farther down by a large tear-stained face on a television screen behind a torn curtain. From the last landing, one could see into a suite of basement offices: fluorescent lighting, rubber trees, filing cabinets, picture postcards on the wall; quite a number of people who belonged there and one helpless outsider, who kept moving out of the employees' way; a man's casually knotted tie, a woman's loose hair, branches of winter jasmine on the windowsill gave the place a homey look. The climate seemed to have grown warmer from landing to landing: high up on the bare rock, icicles as thick as pillars; here below, along with the usual box trees and spruce hedges, the gardens revealed an occasional palm trunk or a glistening round laurel tree, protected to be sure by plastic sheeting. Thus the writer, confident of being unobserved, made, as it were, his entrance into the

21]

city. His goal was a restaurant, not so much because he was hungry or thirsty as because he felt the need to sit in a public place and be waited on for a while; after the long hours alone in his room, he even felt that he had it coming to him.

ON REACHING ground level, he avoided the crowded thoroughfares by means of a detour through the back courtyards, which formed a wide arc around the inner city. One such courtyard, belonging to a school, merged with a second, that of the museum, which in turn debouched into the courtyard of a monastery, from which a passage led to a cemetery that was left unlocked and served exclusively as a park. Since all the buildings were of the same type and the successive courtyards were of roughly the same shape and size, one had the impression that all this was a single compound, cut off from the rest of the world, a city within the city, and that each courtyard led one deeper into a city with no rear exit. For some moments, at the sight of a pump house with a bulbiform wooden roof, the writer thought he was back in Moscow, where he had once spent a whole afternoon in a hidden precinct of this kind, advancing from passage to passage, each more spacious and more open to silence than the last, and then in some far distant place, sitting alone on a long bench watching the children in a sheltered concrete play area, and finally, in the innermost courtyard, a kind of lawn studded with birches, washing his face and hands at an outdoor tap. Surprisingly, it was almost exclusively at times when he was writing that he was able to divest the city he lived in of its limits. Then little became big; names lost their meaning; the light-colored sand in the cracks between cobblestones became the foothills of a dune; a pallid blade of grass became part of a savanna. In one of the schoolrooms a class was still in progress; only the teacher was visible, standing on a platform and waving his arms in front of a shiny blackboard. The base of the museum was decorated with marble reliefs, showing pairs of dolphins swimming toward or away from each other. In the courtyard of the monastery a monk, wearing sandals in spite of the cold, was pruning a cherry tree, and in the cemetery there were not only Latin but Greek inscriptions as well.

The series of enclosed courtyards widened into a procession of open squares. These, too, merged with one another, each a kind of forecourt to the next and larger one—which was always unpredictable; you turned the corner of a church, a public building, or a mere newspaper stand and there it was. But the last and largest of the squares, despite the colonnade at its entrance, had none of the quality of a main square: it consisted of unpaved, yellow clay and sloped gently toward the center, as evidenced by the radial grooves that the rain had gouged out of the ground. From square to square the writer had slackened his pace, and now he stopped. It seemed to him that he was not going away from his work but that it was accompanying him; that, now far from his desk, he was still at work. But what does "work" mean? Work, he thought, is something in which material is next to nothing, structure almost everything; something that rotates on its axis without the help of a flywheel; something whose elements hold one another in suspense; something open and accessible to all, which cannot be worn out by use.

At that point, the writer almost broke into a run. Although the square, only a stone's throw from the river, was the lowest point in the city, he crossed it in a long diagonal, as if it had been a high plateau. The ice crackled under the soles of his shoes, a delicate sound, which quickly spread over the entire surface. The ground was covered with the needles of the Christmas trees that had been sold year after year on this square; stamped into the clay, they themselves had long been clay-yellow. Tomorrow, perhaps, the whole square would be filled with one more pseudo-forest of spruce and fir saplings, through which it would be almost impossible to find one's way.

He couldn't help noticing how shaky he was when he asked for a paper at the newsstand in the arcade leading to the river. He could hardly finish his sentence, and when the change was held out to him he had difficulty taking it. Buying a paper, he said to himself for the hundredth time, had been his first mistake of the day; he resolved that he would just leaf through it, if possible while walking, and then throw it into a trash can. Just glancing at the headlines made him momentarily speechless; in response to the vendor's small talk, the best he could manage was a nod. Seized with a sudden hatred of mankind, he winced when accidentally grazed by a passerby, and looked to one side to avoid speaking to an acquaintance who had recently told him the story of his life; by way of self-justification he "blacked out." As a rule, these blackouts were put on.

On the river bridge he encountered the wind, and with it he went on. Here under the great open vault the air was perceptibly colder than in the courtyards and on the squares. Tatters of mist floated over the almost black water, and in his thoughts ice floes crashed together as they had one glacial winter; it had then been so cold on the bridge that he had literally been obliged to take flight. And in much the same way he relived a summer incident: the river had overflowed its banks, and he saw a little boy running back and forth below the river wall; he had thought the child was playing because of the way he hopped while running; the rushing water prevented the writer from hearing the child, but then he saw by the movements of the child's lips that he was shouting for help. He had fallen off the wall. Again the writer's shoulders felt the strain of pulling the child up; and again, looking across at the deserted Winter Promenade, he saw the little figure in short trousers, running away with flying hair beneath the summer foliage.

In the middle of the bridge, the writer stopped and leaned against the rail. The flagpole holes were empty. Downstream, the horizon gleamed in the strong light; that church steeple in the distance belonged to one of the villages. The many city bridges, one behind the other, all seemed to be on the same level, and the writer had the impression that the cars on the second bridge and the railroad train on the third were moving over the busy footbridge in the foreground. At the bends in the river the dividing line between land and water seemed accentuated by a shimmering. In the midst of the traffic the evening bells were ringing in the weekend, and the sound hung long in the air; all the vehicles in the city seemed to start up again after stopping for a moment, and the gulls above the bridge resumed their apparently interrupted cries.

Making his way upstream on the opposite shore, the writer thought he would keep walking for a long time. Wasn't it just habit that made one stop for food or rest? Here at the water's edge, the waves communicated their strength to him. He was seized with a yearning—after all these years, the word still had meaning—to live again in the foreign metropolises where, even when walking about alone, he knew that a few people in the inner and outer districts were concerned, each in his own way, with the same questions, and were pursuing the same aims, as himself; he had not wanted to meet these doubles, he was content to share the ground under their feet, the wind, the weather, daybreak and nightfall with them. Why was it so hard to imagine that there might be such people in the cities of his homeland? Why in this country did he tend to believe the anecdote about the two writers, one of whom had moved out of his apartment solely because the other passed below his windows day after day?

And now, on the same riverbank as before, he actually ran into the old man who had introduced himself as a "colleague." All he knew about the man was that he had been first a teacher, then a soldier in the war, then again a teacher, and that now in his retirement he wrote poems. As though he had been waiting a long time for this opportunity, the old man began at once, in lieu of greeting, to recite one of them in a loud, almost threatening voice, and when the poem was finished proceeded to talk without changing his rhythm or enunciation. This of course made it impossible for the writer to take in what he was saying. He heard only the words, not their meaning. But he saw the old man's naked eyes, wide open as though blind; the discolored irises, with rings of color only at the edges; and a pulsating in the pouch under one eye. When they separated and the writer looked after his "colleague," words were still pouring from him in a high-pitched, seemingly endless hum which might have meant enthusiasm or might have meant protest.

The restaurant was by the river; it was almost empty and the writer found a seat with a view of the water: the current seemed swift, as though the river had just burst through the mountains. The writer had the feeling that he was still walking across bridges among the silhouettes of the passersby. Before turning his attention to the newspaper, he took a deep breath and imprinted the most distant horizon on his mind to steady himself. But again it was no use. With the first sentence, he lost all power of thought. He often tried to persuade himself that it was his duty to keep informed by reading newspapers. (During the period of his vow not to read the papers, he had missed the news that some of his heroes and saints had died, and found out when it was too late for reflection.) But actually his thumbing through the papers was an addiction. He seldom read a complete paragraph; at the most he would race through a paper, article after article, in a state of combined frenzy and catalepsy. He kept commanding himself to start all over again and absorb the whole of at least one story. Then, however, it became apparent to him that in merely glancing through it he had taken in the entire content; but, alas, the story did not, like certain poems, "end deep in his soul"—on the contrary, it left him utterly indifferent. At this point the addict—suffering from an addiction that was not even a pleasure—thought longingly of the months in New York, when a long strike had stopped all newspapers from appearing. There was only a thin bulletin, calling itself *City News*, which in a few lines reported every happening on earth that might have been worth knowing. Every day the writer had studied this *City News* and when "at last!" as most people gasped, great piles of the "international organ" became available at every subway entrance, he deeply regretted the passing of the modest little bulletin. How superfluous all the opinions and special reports, all the columnists and commentators seemed. They left the reader with a buzzing of wasps in his ears. And worst of all were the writers on "cultural" matters, who seldom opened their mouths without delivering an opinion. Yes, he had recognized now and then that criticism could be an art in its own right, the art of finding the right angle from which to look at a work—one might also speak of it as "vision" and the conscientious elaboration of this vision. But as a rule, such pages were at best filled-in schemas and at worst imposture, in which appreciation has long since given way to easily discernible ulterior motives; where criticism has been crowded out by machination. In the writer's youthful dreams, literature had been the freest of all countries and the thought of it the only possible way of escaping from the vileness and submissions of daily life to a proud equality, and no doubt many had pursued some such dream. But now all of them, as he saw it, were stuck in the most despotic of all petty principalities, either clustered in unthinking cronyism or dispersed by deadly enmities; even the most obstreperous among them had quickly degenerated into diplomats and let themselves be governed by undiscriminating commissars in whom the lust for power had taken the place of taste. Once the writer was at the deathbed of a fellow writer. What interested his dying colleague more than anything else was what was being said in the cultural section of the newspapers. Did these battles of opinion take his mind off his illness by infuriating him or making him laugh? Did they put him in mind of an eternal repetition, preferable after all to what was in store for him? There was more to it than that. Even in his hopeless situation, far-removed as he was from the editorial offices, he was their prisoner; more than his nearest and dearest, the critics and editors were the object of his dreams; and in the intervals when he was free from pain, he would ask, since by then he was incapable of reading, what one publication or another had said about some new book. The intrigues, and the almost pleasurable fury they aroused in the sufferer—who saw through them—brought a kind of world, a certain permanence into the sickroom, and the man at his bedside understood his vituperating or silently nodding friend as well as if it had been his own self lying there. But later, when the end was near and the dying man still insisted on having opinions read out to him from the latest batch of newspapers, the witness vowed that he would never let things come to such a pass with him as they had with his image and likeness. Never again would he involve himself in this circuit of classifications and judgments, the substance of which was almost exclusively the playing off of one writer or school against another. Over the years since then, he had derived pride and satisfaction from staying on the outside and carrying on by his own strength rather than at the expense of rivals. The mere thought of returning to the circuit or to any of the persistently warring cliques made him feel physically ill. Of course, he would never get entirely away from them, for even today, so long after his vow, he suddenly caught sight of a word that he at first mistook for his name. But today at least he was glad—as he would not have been years ago—to have been mistaken. Lulled in security, he leafed through the local section and succeeded in giving his mind to every single news item.

When at last he raised his eyes from his paper, he experienced a violent feeling of loss. The waitress's little boy had been sitting all the while over his homework at the table beside the kitchen door. Instead of looking at the child for any length of time, he had intermittently registered its presence. And now the place at the table was empty. On the chair where the child had sat, tracing letters in his copy-book that he would show to his mother from time to time when she passed, there was only his bright-colored schoolbag.

The writer's newspaper reading seemed to have destroyed his field of vision; the edge of the neighboring table no longer presented a line. With a jolt he thrust his paper aside. Then, seeing that in spite of himself he kept squinting at it out of the corners of his eyes, he covered it with the menu. Finally, catching himself blindly reading the menu, he removed both newspaper and menu from his line of sight by putting them on a chair seat under the table.

He thought of leaving but remained sitting, alone with a glass of wine, from which he took a sip at intervals. He didn't want to go out in that condition, with dulled senses that made him incapable of perceiving or thinking about anything. More and more people came in, but he saw only legs and torsos, not a single face. Luckily he was unobserved. The waitress had probably known his name at one time, but had long since forgotten it. For a moment the river outside sparkled—no, the sparkling was only a little spot in the water; then a flock of sparrows flew into a tree on the bank, their many outspread wings joined to form a cloud that vanished at once from the sky. A moment later the tiny birds sat motionless in the branches; motionless, too, were the crows in the crown of the neighboring tree and even the normally restless gulls on the railings of the bridge. Though there was not a flake in sight, snow seemed to be falling on them. And through this living picture—the barely perceptible movement of wings, the barely open beaks, the twinkle of tiny eyes—the summer landscape in which he had set the story he was writing at the time opened up to him. White flowers no larger than shirt buttons rained down from the elder bushes, the fruit pods of the walnut trees were beginning to fill out. The jet of the fountain met the cumulus cloud overhead. In a wheat field near which sheep were grazing, the ears of grain crackled in the heat; the city streets were covered with poplar fluff so light and airy that one could see through to the asphalt; and over the grass in the park there passed a droning which became a humming when the bumblebee that went with it vanished into a flower. The swimmer in the river plunged his head into the water for the first time that year and once again the air and the sun and the feel of his nostrils gave the writer a sense of temporary reprieve. Once it had been the other way around: one summer, while daydreaming a winter story, he had reached into the tall grass for a snowball, wanting to throw it playfully at the cat.

FORTIFIED BY these images, he stepped out into the open; he now felt able to continue on his way out of town straight through the busy street which—because he had never seen an unaccompanied individual there, and because as a rule he, too, lost himself by the time he had gone halfway—he privately called Mob Street. Over the years he had tried repeatedly to see this segment of street as a place like any other and to describe it with its bends, bumps, and points of view—as though such "localization" were a writer's business—and time and again, long before the end of the street, he had silently crept off into some arcade. But, this time, wasn't it a good sign that he had passed a bookstore with his head in the air, so to speak, instead of glancing involuntarily at the display window to see if any of his books were in it? (He had often imagined that he had shaken off the habit and then, still cheered by that proud thought, automatically turned his head in the direction of the window.)

It was already getting dark in the long street with its many bends that cut off the view and its tall houses with overhanging roofs, while the strip of sky overhead was still bright like an afterimage of the street below. In shop after shop, the same Christmas music interrupted by loudspeaker voices celebrating articles of consumption in a litany consisting almost entirely of numbers. People flowing in the opposite direction seemed completely wrapped up in themselves, yet the writer was not overlooked. At the very beginning of the street he was assaulted by the collective glance of a group of young people, a glance not of recognition but of incomprehension or even hostility. He surmised that they had just come from school, where they had been made to discuss the meaning or purpose or source of a literary passage and that when at last restored to freedom they had resolved instantly and unanimously never to open a book again and to look with contempt on all those responsible for such torture. And he couldn't blame them, for, though he often regretted it, he was not one of those, be they demagogues or bards, who spoke up boldly, sure of their mission—on the contrary, when called upon to speak he would all but lose his voice; at best he would be carried away by his words, and later, if the result was published, he would be seized with terror or shame—he would even feel guilty, as if he had broken a taboo. Was all this rooted in his own nature, or was it the people of this particular country and their particular brand of German, in which, if there had ever been a tradition, it had long since gone out of existence? This collective evil eye, in any case, made him feel like part of a film, being shot and projected at the same time, of himself walking down the street—his eyes were the camera and his ears the sound recorder. Some of the passersby stopped short, obviously wondering where they could have seen his face. Wasn't that the face on the "Wanted" poster in the post office, the only picture that had not yet been crossed out? A few, still puzzled in the distance, smiled at him as they came closer, not out of friendliness, but because they at last knew where to place him; but a moment later their faces froze, because, unlike an actor they had seen in some role or a politician they had watched on TV, he was not someone they could connect with anything. Just once, halfway down the street, one of the passersby seemed to know something about him. In passing, for the barest instant, he encountered, or so at least it seemed to him, the glance of a reader. Afterward he couldn't even have said if it was a man or a woman; one or the other, he felt, belonged to a sex apart, and this sex, he thought, was recognizable by the eyes which showed gratitude, wished him well, believed in him, and unwaveringly trusted him to go on with his work. But this very experience, brief as it was, gave a jolt to the film which up until then had been flowing along uneventfully. Encouraged by the earnestness of those reader's eyes, the writer, grown overconfident, began searching the crowd for other kindred spirits (where one member of this rare species had shown himself, there was bound to be a second and a third!)—and from that moment on, an enemy army was marching toward him. He saw himself confronted by dagger-eye after dagger-eye, secondhand readers who hated books but, because they were well-informed, thought they knew all about them, as they did about everything else in heaven and earth. But wasn't their malignance a mere figment of his imagination? No, the experience wasn't new to him—they really were ready to leap, to go for his throat, for he stood for everything they detested: daydreams, hand-made writing, dissent, and ulti- mately art. Just wait till I get you in front of my mudguards on the open road; till I get you in front of my ticket window; till I get you in the dock at my courthouse; till you lie chained to your hospital bed and I, at last, get the job of giving you your daily injections . . . Yet none of these like-minded people had conspired with any of the others; none of those who fired off that look at him knew that his pre- decessor had done the exact same thing. All these so very divergent people—young and old, city dwell- ers and rustics, dwellers in the past and devotees of progress—had only one thing in common and that was their obvious hatred, which the writer—re- minded of one of Chekhov's stories, the hero of which says of an upright woman, who respected only those who contributed directly and tangibly to social progress: "She disliked me because I was a land- scape painter"—called "hatred of landscape paint- ers." He stood up to the advance guard of the enemy, he may even have mollified them by pretending, as he often did, to be immersed in a silent inner mono- logue. But then so many stepped into the breach that all his powers forsook him, even the power to project a wordless conciliatory look, which he regarded as his special gift; incapable of grasping the overall context of the film, he was assaulted by disconnected details—for instance, he mistook a pair of glasses, bobbing up and down between someone's fingers, for handcuffs. And in all those identically creased foreheads and bared teeth he seemed to see his own image, very different from the way he had looked on the open squares. Surprised by the stare of a bunch of keys held in someone's fist, he looked down at his own hand in the belief that the person armed with the keys was himself . . . He tried looking up at the sky, but the milling crowd was repeated in the heights; and when he lowered his eyes, all he could see, instead of the human footprints often discernible in the asphalt, were manhole covers, every few steps another, inscribed with the words SANITATION DEPARTMENT. Nor was it possible, on either side, to look into a workroom or a home. Shop shouldered shop, and because of the way they were lined up, all their brightly colored merchandise looked like dummy displays, while the mannequins, for all their exaggerated flashing of teeth, gave the impression of living beings. In the arcades, the eyes of the cripples and beggars were searching for the man responsible for their misfortune; and on the upper stories, deserted in contrast to the milling crowd down below, there wasn't so much as a plant to be seen, not a dog or a cat quietly sitting there, not even a globe (or rather just one, and two children, hardly more than babies, visible down to the neck, looking at it; profile to profile, quite motionless, they were clutching each other's hair). The film, so smoothly flowing at first, did more than jump; it broke off. But the voices and sounds aimed at the writer from out of the hubbub could be heard all the more clearly. A surprising number of people, who had been quietly thinking about him and wanted to have him in their sights, were now in the street. If they hadn't been thinking about him, would they have been so ready to fire off their pronouncements at the top of their voices? True, they never once addressed him; they spoke into the air or to their companions, as often as not in a whisper, so that nothing could be heard but the questions: "Who?" "What did you say?" "What about him?" "What would you like to do?" Even those representing themselves as couples, holding hands or even with their arms around each other, broke apart the moment they caught sight of him and, visibly relieved at not having to play "couple" anymore, began to talk about him. Not only did their words pertain to him, but certain sounds as well, even a sucking in of air.

43]

While one sang a sequence of sounds deliberately out of tune, a second yawned with might and main, a third cleared his throat, the fourth jabbed the sidewalk with his metal-tipped cane, the next snorted, and then came a chorus of scraping stiletto heels. Toward the end of the street—not bad to have made it that far—the writer was decisively defeated. A voice called him from behind, he looked around involuntarily, and his picture was taken. A man in black barred his way and announced solemnly: "I have been following your output." And finally, still another man, without looking at him, demanded "an autograph for my child." While the writer complied (wishing, to be sure, that he had a third, mechanical arm for the purpose), it seemed to him that he was no longer a writer as he had been during the hour after work, but was merely playing the part of a writer in a forced, ridiculous way; wasn't it ridiculous, for instance, that when giving the man his autograph he had had to reflect a moment before remembering his name? On the other hand, he said to himself, it served him right for allowing his face to become known. If it were possible in his profession to start all over again, he wouldn't allow a single picture to be taken of him.

Looking back at the scene of his discomfiture from the road into which the street broadened, he thought of the author who was said, every time a book of his appeared, to be going "from triumph to triumph," imagined that there were no more readers left in the whole country, and recalled his dream about a book which—like a ship that had just set sail—was full of bookmarks, all of which were gone when he awoke.

AFTER THAT, it was a pleasure to be surrounded by the crashing and pounding of the traffic. Strange how easily his composure could be shaken after all the years and how, after long, often enthusiastic work that made him glow inwardly, there was still no certainty in his life. And now another of his vows: To change his afternoon occupations until his present work was finished. Until then he wouldn't open a single newspaper and he would avoid this street, the whole city center in fact. Straight out to the periphery, that's the place for me! Or why not stay home in his room, where he belonged and where he experienced neither hunger nor thirst nor any need for human company—where he could still his hunger and thirst and become integrated with the

[46

procession of passersby by merely meditating, observing, recording his observations? Wouldn't the last light of day at this very moment be shining on the paper in his typewriter and on the pencils around it, pointing in all directions, while on the hill nearby the signals for the evening planes blinked at regular intervals? The whole house, steps, banister, and all, seemed to have been left high and dry; it was as though the plants in the entrance with their few winter blossoms were asking to be looked at.

The road soon became an arterial highway. At the crossing, back to back, hung two crucified Christs, the one facing into the city, the other toward the periphery. On the bench below, surrounded by plastic bags, sat a gray-haired man, shouting into the traffic noise, haranguing all mankind. In passing, the writer heard something like "You swine, looking for the old city of ruins, aren't you, when you yourselves have destroyed it!" Invigorated by the shrill voice behind him, listening to it as long as possible, the writer strode briskly onward, convinced that he had discovered, in the trunk of a recently pollarded plane tree, the turrets and battlements of the madman's "city of ruins."

Relieved when the driver of a car that stopped abruptly in front of him merely asked for directions, the writer hoped for more people who didn't know the way; he would gladly have helped them all. A knot of dangerous-looking customers by the side of the road proved to be waiting for the bus. From that point on, there was little to be seen but gas stations and warehouses, with more and more wasteland in between. As he looked back toward the city, the gulls circling high above the roofs gave him a sense of the river, which he could not see. The trees by the roadside were followed by hedges and thickets full of little white snowberries. How varied the summer's green had been and how varied now was the gray of the winter branches—the greens easier to distinguish from a distance, the grays from close at hand.

In a thicket shading from one gray to another, the writer caught sight of a bright-colored form. At first glance he took it for an overturned advertising dummy, but then, by the bend of the fingers, he knew it was a living person. There lay an old woman, almost hairless, her eyes closed. She was stretched out prone, not on the ground, but on a tangle of branches that sagged under her weight. Only the tips of her shoes touched the ground; her whole body

slanted, making the writer think, partly because of
the outstretched arms, of an airplane that had made
an emergency landing in a treetop. Her stockings
were twisted and across her forehead there was a
bleeding cut, made no doubt by a thorn. She must
have been lying there a long time and might have
stayed a lot longer, for pedestrians seldom came that
way. The writer was unable to lift the heavy body—
which was surprisingly warm—out of the thicket.
But his efforts attracted attention, several cars
stopped, and without asking questions helpers came
running. Someone pushed a coat under the woman's head, and they all gathered around her on the
footpath, waiting for an ambulance. Though no one
knew anyone else, they—even the foreigners among
them—stood chatting like former neighbors, whom
a splendid accident had brought together after all
these years. An inspired namelessness prevailed.
Nor did the victim, who was conscious, supply a
name. She stared fixedly at the writer out of large,
bright eyes. She knew neither her name nor her
address, nor how she had got tangled up in these
brambles along the highway. She was wearing a
nightgown and bedroom slippers under a dressing
gown; the people who had gathered conjectured that
she came from the old people's home and had lost

her way. She spoke the language of the land without dialect, but with an accent suggesting not some far-off region but childhood, as though her childhood language had come back to her after long absence. Actually, her speech consisted only of disjointed syllables or sounds, addressed like her glances exclusively to her discoverer. Speaking incoherently but in a clear voice, she was trying to tell him something important, something that he alone would understand—but that he would understand fully and without difficulty. In a few fragments, unintelligible to the others, she told him the whole story of her life, from her girlhood years to the present. Already in the care of the ambulance, she was still talking to him, urgently, as though entrusting him with a mission. And indeed, when the helpers had gone and he was alone again, it seemed to him that he knew intuitively all there was to know about the confused old woman. Hadn't he always learned more from intuition than from objective knowledge? Looking up at the empty hedge, he foresaw that the heavy body with the bent fingers would be lying there time and again, forever and ever. "O holy intuitions, stay with me."

As he was walking across country, snow began to fall. To his mind "snow" and "begin" belonged together more than almost any other two experiences; the "first snow" was rather like the first brimstone butterfly in the early spring, the first cuckoo call in May, the first plunge into the water in summer, the first bite into an autumn apple. Yet, over the years, the expectation had become stronger than the experience itself. And today the flakes that were barely grazing him had seemed in anticipation to strike the middle of his forehead.

As he was crossing the open fields by his usual diagonal path, his just acquired namelessness, favored by the snowfall and his walking alone, took on substance. This experience of namelessness might at one time have been termed a liberation from limits or from the self. To be at last wholly outside, among things, was a kind of enthusiasm, one felt one's eyebrows arching. Yes, to be rid of his name was ground for enthusiasm; like the legendary Chinese painter, he felt himself disappearing into the picture—he saw, for example, the claw arms of a trolleybus brush like an insect's feelers over a single tall fir tree in the distance. Strange that so many people, when thinking themselves alone and unobserved, reminded him, with their grumbling, throat clearing, and puffing, of those crackling trolleybuses, which really ought to be brought back into use, and that with him it was usually the contrary: it was only when nameless and alone with things that he really started functioning. If someone had asked him now what his name was, his answer would have been: "I have no name," and he would have said this so earnestly that the questioner would have understood him at once.

The snow settled first on the middle strip of grass; it looked as though birch branches had been laid on the road, one after another, and so on to the horizon. In a bramblebush, single crystals would balance on thorns and then encircle them like ruffs. Though there was no one to be seen, the writer had the impression at every step that he was walking in the traces of someone who had been there before. This place at the edge of the city corresponded to what he had been doing all day long at his desk. He wanted to run, but instead he stopped on a bridge across a brook. An ascending plane filled the air with its sound; the grass at the bottom of the brook wriggled. The snow, no longer gliding flakes but little hard balls, plunged deep into the brook, as acorns do in the fall; at the same time, the sliding and crashing of village curling stones reached him from far off through the twilight, and with them the writer's forebears came alive to him for a moment. His shoes were pleasantly heavy shoes, they held his ankles snug and warm, and as though these were the first comfortable walking shoes in his life, he addressed a hymn of praise to them: "With your predecessors I was always in danger of rushing headlong. You are the right shoes for me, because in you I feel myself stamping the earth, and above all because you are the brake shoes I need. You know of course that slowness is the only illumination I have ever had."

At the edge of the city, he sat down on the bench in a bus shelter. The more erect he sat and the more slowly he breathed, the warmer he felt. The falling snow scraped against the wall of the shelter. Like the bench, it was made of gray weathered wood; the back wall was covered with a thick layer of tattered posters and meaningless scraps of white lettering. Just behind the bus terminus, a road turned off to the Autobahn. In the brightly lit snack bar at the fork, a man with a mustache and a linen chef's hat, which only on closer scrutiny turned out to be paper, was moving about irresolutely amid mist, steam, and tongues of flame in the absence of customers; behind him, beside the tin cans and paper cups, an old-fashioned wall clock with curved hands and Roman numerals. The motordrome for student drivers on the man-made hill beyond the Autobahn was closed for the winter, as was the nearby camping ground. The few poplars farther on, each with the silhouette of a bird in it, were a vestige of a tree-lined avenue. Then came a scraggly meadow, into which jutted the concrete surface of a former military road still bearing the imprint of tank treads. This whole area at the edge of the city, with the concentrated din of traffic coming from all directions, struck him as a place one could live in, comparable to the region on the fringe of dreams, where he would gladly have dwelt forever. He would have liked to live in one of the scattered cottages with a back garden merging directly with the meadow, or over there above the warehouse, where the yellow light of a desk lamp had just come on. Pencils, a table, a chair. Freshness and strength emanated from edges, as in an everlasting age of pioneering.

Suddenly he felt the need to read something in this particular place. All he had on him was the picture postcard from America. But, despite the harsh street lighting, he was unable to decipher his one-time friend's writing, which seemed more and more to imitate the zigzags of his inexplicable wanderings around the continent—on every card a different postmark. While the pictures continued to show more or less identical samples of untrammeled nature, a canyon or a sierra, the last recognizable letters vanished from the text. Only recently, parallel series of dots, semicircles, and wavy lines had suggested arabesques; now the lines had lost all shape and were so far apart that it was hard to conceive of any connection between them. Only the address and the "As ever" and signature at the end were still written as plainly as before. What the obscure scribble communicated to the addressee was a furious effort, manifested by the pressure of the pen, the split lines, and the blots—as though the writer had repeatedly and vainly assaulted the paper. But this mutilated cuneiform, in which all trace of the human hand had been extinguished, also expressed something else: a threat, an omen of death aimed at the addressee.

On the city side of the shelter, a last little side road led to a housing development. His eyesight sharpened by his attempts to decipher the postcard, the writer raised his head. A patch of daytime sky could still be seen in the traffic mirror on the corner, a small bright rectangle in the surrounding darkness. In it the houses of the development, all with steep roofs, seemed greatly reduced in size and at the same time raised, with concave pagoda-like roofs. The street itself, which was straight in reality, seemed to bend and spread out, and where it came to an end in the yard between two houses presented a discernible perspective, as though it led still farther. The mirror image had no season: the snow in the air could have been flying seeds, the snow on the ground could have been fallen blossoms. The rounding of the image gave emptiness a radiance, and gave the objects in this emptiness—the glass-recycling center, the garbage cans, the bicycle stands—a holiday feel, as though in looking at them one emerged into a clearing. The animated beings in this image also seemed transformed. The mirror brought the grown-ups and children outside the grocery store closer together and accentuated the differences in their sizes. Standing there quietly together, they had time; and on the road, instead of a car, a single enormous bird appeared: circling out of the brightness, it flew directly at the beholder (and passed him in the darkness, tiny and twittering). The rectangular playground at the edge of the development was transformed into an oval. At the moment it was not in use, but in the emptiness a swing was still moving; the writer watched it until the aftereffect of the child's motion had dwindled to a mere trembling of ropes in the snowy wind. "Emptiness, my guiding principle. Emptiness, my beloved."

THOUGH NOTHING much had happened, he felt
that he had seen and experienced enough that day—
thus securing his tomorrow. For today he required
no more, no sight or conversation, and above all
nothing new. Just to rest, to close his eyes and ears;
just to inhale and exhale would be effort enough.
He wished it was bedtime. Enough of being in the
light and out of doors; he wanted to be in the dark,
in the house, in his room. But he had also had
enough of being alone; he felt, as time passed, that
he was experiencing every variety of madness and
that his head was bursting. He recalled how, years
ago, when it had been his habit to take afternoon
walks on lonely bypaths, a strange uneasiness had
taken possession of him, leading him to believe that

[58

he had dissolved into the air and ceased to exist.
Thus, wishing on the one hand to have no further
experience that day, and on the other hand to make
sure that, far from being out of his mind, he was,
as he had discovered time and again in company,
one of the few more or less sane individuals at large,
he went to a bar at the edge of town which he privately thought of as the "gin mill." It was a place
he frequented now and then during his working
months. He even had his place there, in a niche near
the jukebox, offering a view of an intersection and
the used-car lot behind it. But today, when he had
pushed through the crowd, he found that his niche
had been bricked over. For a moment he thought
he had come to the wrong place, but then he recognized, one after another, the faces that could be
associated only with this particular room, with this
smoke and artificial light. (If he had met them in-
dividually by day in the city, he would not have
known where to place them.) As he made room for
himself and looked around, he recalled certain particulars concerning each one of them. Not a few had
told him the whole story of their lives, most of which
he had forgotten by the next day. What he remembered were certain turns of phrase, exclamations,
gestures, intonations. The first had once blurted out:

59]

"When I'm right, I get excited; when I'm wrong, I lie"; the second went to Mass every Sunday because it always gave him the cold shivers; the third, a woman, referred to each of her rapidly changing lovers as her "fiancé"; the fourth, spraying his listeners with saliva, had cried out: "I'm lost!"; the fifth was in the habit of saying that he had achieved all his aims in life—what the writer particularly remembered about him was that he had once touched the writer's wrist, a kind of nudge one might have called it, with a tenderness possible only for a man on the brink of despair. This group of people was as nondescript as the bar itself. In one of the two rooms, stag's antlers side by side with a color photo of a Chinese junk; in the other, a stucco ceiling fit for a villa over a slightly raised rustic dance floor. The usual stolid-looking habitués' table in one corner was always occupied by the same people, but they had nothing in common: the salesman in the silk suit sat next to the former owner in felt slippers, who now lived in a room on the upper floor; his neighbor was a veteran of the Foreign Legion who had changed into the uniform of a security guard; and his opposite was an unemployed ship's steward, invariably clad in a tracksuit, accompanied by his fiancée, a nurse (under her chair, a motorcycle helmet). Everyone else in the two rooms might just as well have been sitting at that table. The one thing they probably had in common was that every one of them had thought of writing a book of at least a thousand pages about his life, "beginning at birth!" But if asked about the content, they would refer as a rule to some trifling incident, to something they had seen from the window, a hut burning in the night, rivers of mud in the roadway after a rainfall, but often with deep feeling, as though these trifles stood for a whole long life.

The writer's evening in the gin mill began well for him. The others pretended not to notice him, but at the same time they perceptibly made room for him, wherever he happened to be. They had come to realize that he came here, not to observe them or to "collect material," but most likely because his existence was as marginal as theirs. As he pressed the buttons of the jukebox after a day spent looking for words, he felt relieved to be operating with mere numbers. Even before the song started— what he wanted now was a song sung by a woman's voice—the machine communicated its buzzing and vibration to him. Although he heard very little of the music through the noise, he occasionally recognized a particular interval, and that was enough. One of the cardplayers kept looking up at the invisible heavens, while the others, firmly gripping their cards, kept him in the corners of their eyes. The commuters at the table by the door were waiting for the last bus back to their villages. The one unoccupied table had a RESERVED sign on it; it was even set in anticipation of guests who evidently had something to celebrate, for the owner's daughter, who had learned the trade in a very different establishment, conjured up large napkins which opened like fans as she set them down. The cat, which was sleeping between the potted plants on the windowsill, was so much like his own that for a moment the writer thought it had come here ahead of him. Through the opening between the window curtains he could watch the steady flow of evening buses, jam-packed with seated and standing passengers. And through the misted panes he was able for an instant to see each individual face in its diversity, and in that same instant he remembered how once, looking up from his paper after long immersion, he had seen every single leaf of the tree outside his window and at the same time all the leaves together, leaf for leaf, shape for shape. A summer of joyful work, and now in his imagining he unfolded a slow procession of images:

from the stone stairway flanked by fern fronds, all
unrolled except for one with the coiled shape of a
crosier, to the high plateau with the cloud shadows,
where the buzzing of bees in a tree suggested the
unisonal humming of a human chorus, from there
to a road where a cyclist, blinded by the fly in his
eye, braked abruptly, and past the junction of the
three paths, down to the lake, black and deserted
before the storm, on the shore of which an old man
in a straw hat was sitting with his barefoot grandson
in the shelter of a kiosk when a wind squall sent a
great icicle crashing at their feet, and in the end a
glowworm circled through the night-black garden
and flew into the dark, open house, lighting up the
corners . . . in one of which a grasshopper was sitting.
Did such imagining in processions of forms take him
out of present reality? Or did it, on the contrary,
disentangle and clarify the present, form connec-
tions between isolated particulars, and set his imprint on them all, the dripping beer tap and the
steadily flowing water faucet behind the bar, the
unknown figures in the room and the silhouettes
outside? Yes, when he gave himself over to these
fantasies, the things and people present appeared to
him all at once with no need to be counted, and like
the leaves in that summer tree joined to form a large

number. But now, face to face with this present, he realized what it lacked: the entrance of beauty in the form of a woman—not specifically to meet him (for since his time on the frontiers of language it was almost as though he had left his body there), but to join everyone in the room. Once such an apparition had actually stood in the doorway. Looking for a telephone? Wanting to buy cigarettes? To ask the way into town? At the sight of her the whole dreary gin-mill community had come to life. Without lowering their voices or explicitly looking in her direction, each one had tried, while beauty was there, to show his best and noblest side, if only to his immediate neighbor. Even after she had gone— though not a word was said about her—those left behind remained united in a kind of awe; time and again, with a rare unanimity, their eyes lit up. That was a long time ago, but even now he—he alone?— cast an occasional glance at the door, in the hope that the unknown woman would reappear. She never did, and today his grief at her staying away almost swelled to indignation. The door remained closed. Instead, a drunk made his way from the bar through clouds of smoke which occasionally hid him from view. Arrived at the table, he stared from high above, as though he had only one eye, first at the writer's notebook, then at the writer himself, pushed into the seat beside him, and immediately started talking. As he spoke, his face came so close as to lose its contours; only his violently twitching eyelids, the dotted bow tie under his chin, and a cut on his forehead that must have bled recently remained distinct. He stank prodigiously and not only of sweat; he seemed to have accumulated all the foul smells in the world from carrion to sulfur. Not a single word of what he was saying came through to the writer, not even when he held his ear close to the speaker's mouth. Yet, to judge by the movements of his lips and tongue, he was not speaking a foreign language. Not even the sibilants accentuated in whispering were audible. Now and then the speaker would stroke his own cheek and from time to time he would stop talking and catch his breath, producing a long-drawn-out sound resembling that of a wind instrument being tuned. When asked to speak more loudly, he would seem to perk up—give a lift to his shoulders and stretch his neck—after which the flow of words would go on, as voicelessly as before. Though he neither looked at the writer nor assailed him with gestures, it was obvious that what he had to say was addressed exclusively to him. He was trying to tell him something important. For a time the listener actually felt that he understood what was being said to him; he would nod, apparently at the right places (for the other smiled as though in receipt of corroboration). And then suddenly—for once this word, often so thoughtlessly used, is peculiarly apt—suddenly the writer lost the secret thread, known only to the two of them, and at the same time, just as suddenly and inexplicably, he lost the nexus with his next morning's writing, which he thought he had secured that afternoon and without which he would be unable to carry on with his work. He had thought out every single sentence down to the last, all that remained was to put them in the right order—and now suddenly all these words had lost their validity; indeed, it seemed to him, thinking back, that everything he had done since the summer, everything that had given strength to his shoulders during the last hours, had instantly been pronounced null and void. At first he put the blame on the smoke in the gin mill—it impeded not only his breathing but also his imagining—and went to the toilet, hoping that the coolness, the tiles, and the running water would restore his composure. But there, too, he remained inwardly mute. It was as though his work, an airy castle only a short while before, had never been, and when he looked in the mirror he saw his enemy. Reluctantly, he went back to the table, a prisoner of the inaudible man who, having waited sitting up straight, his chest thrown out imperiously, instantly resumed his obscure flow, as though he had been interrupted in midsentence. The writer, who at that point only appeared to be listening, suffered from a frequent nightmare, a dream that came to him only at times when he was writing. Nothing happened in it, its only content was a judgment repeated all through the night: What he had written that day was irrelevant and meaningless; he should never have written it, for to write was criminal; to produce a work of art, a book, was presumption, more damnable than any other sin. Now, in the midst of the "gin-mill people," he had the same feeling of unpardonable guilt, the feeling that he had been banished from the world for all time. But now he was able to question himself systematically—as he could not in his dreams—about his problem, the problem of writing, describing, storytelling. What was his business, the business of a writer? Was there any such business in this century? Was there anyone, for example, whose deeds and sufferings cried out not only to be recorded, catalogued, and publicized in history books but also to be handed down in the form of an epic or perhaps only of a little song? To what god was it still possible to intone a hymn of praise? (And who could still summon up the strength to lament the absence of a god?) Where was the long-reigning sovereign whose rule demanded to be celebrated by something more than gun salutes? Where was his successor, whose accession deserved to be greeted by something more than flashbulbs? Where were the Olympic victors whose homecoming warranted something more than cheers, flag waving, and a flourish of drums? What mass murderers of this century, instead of rising from the pit with each new justification, might be sent back to their hell forever with a single tercet? And how, on the other hand, since the end of the world is no mere fancy but a distinct possibility at any moment, can one just praise the beloved objects of this planet with a stanza or a paragraph about a tree, a countryside, a season? Where, today, was one to look for the "aspect of eternity"? And in view of all this, who could claim to be an artist and to have made a place for himself in the world? In reply to all these questions, the answer came: By isolating myself (how many years ago?) in order to write, I acknowledged my defeat as a social being; I excluded myself from society once and for all. Even if I sit here among the people to

[68

the end, welcomed, embraced, initiated into their secrets, I shall never be one of them.

Strangely pleased with the outcome of this internal dialogue, he pulled himself together and at the same time met the eyes of the man beside him, who was still moving his lips. He had stopped blinking, but the immobility of his gaze was the exact opposite of "resting on something." They had detected the absence of the supposed kindred spirit, and absence meant betrayal. A brief look of contempt was followed by a long turning away. And in turning away, the inaudible interlocutor finally became audible. "You're a weakling," he said, "and a liar." And addressing the whole room, he said on a mournful, deep-chested note: "None of you know who I am." Then, in a twinkling, he grabbed the writer's notebook and covered the still empty pages with a hodgepodge of dots and spirals. That done, he stood up and began to dance, executing figures that seemed to follow the choreography of his scribbles.

The dancer, graceful even in his staggering and stumbling, had vanished one-two-three into the crowd. Now the writer caught sight at the next table of a man whom he called the "legislator," though they had never exchanged a word. The man was younger than the writer, he was always wearing the same sheepskin jacket, he was broad-shouldered, his ears stuck out, and under his high, arched brows his eyes were set so deep in their sockets that they seemed small. His unflagging attentiveness gave him a military air. Yet he was the only one at his table who kept out of fights. Indeed, he moderated them, not by mixing in, but by expressly ignoring them. The others at the table were constantly jostling one another; he alone kept his peace. The look of quiet sorrow that he trained on two neighbors who were exchanging slaps stopped them from going at each other with their fists or possibly drawing knives. Silently he took in detail after detail and had a mute reply for everyone. When he opened his mouth to deliver a short sentence, his constant attentiveness seemed to have set the tone for his voice: never wavering, it laconically disposed of questionable behavior. This man who seldom spoke was the authority in the room; the power he radiated was the power of judgment. His kind of justice, however, was not static, not an unvarying rule; it was different in every instance, it was justice in action, a nascent justice with a wordlessly sympathetic rhythm, which pronounced judgment and at the end discharged the parties into silence. This silent listener with the flashing eyes, which took in a picture of everything, and the broad rolling shoulders that seemed to move in rhythm with whatever was going on in the room: was he not the ideal storyteller?

Had he been watching the legislator for hours or only for a moment? In any case, it now seemed to him that he had been sitting too long in the gin mill, and not for the first time he thought he would never find his way home again. He felt glued to the spot, incapable of movement; it seemed inconceivable that he would ever stand up and "make it" to the door. He would first have to think about each leg of the return journey, as if it were an expedition and the caravan routes, jungle trails, fords, mountain passes, and base camps all had to be mapped out in advance. In his precipitate flight, a billiard cue grazed him, a dog snarled at him, and, lastly, the belt of his coat got caught on the door handle.

OUT IN THE STREET, he rebuttoned and retied everything from his jacket to his shoes. If he had now, as he planned a short while ago, hurled his notebook like a discus, it would have landed at his feet. The snow had stopped falling, the sky was covered with clouds. The snow was deep and firm; the dripping from the street lamps had gouged out pockmark patterns, in which the madman's "city of ruins" was repeated. As in childhood the writer had crouched down over rain trails in the dust, he now stooped over these craters; when he stuck his hand into them, the snow burned his skin as healingly as nettles had done in years gone by.

His eyes on the ground, he headed straight for the city despite his impulse to take the opposite course from all the people moving in the same direction, or at least to walk faster or more slowly than they. This was the niggling hour, when his thoughts turned not to work but to his daily omissions: again he had failed to write the promised letter; again someone's manuscript had gone unread; again he had neglected to put his tax papers in order; he hadn't paid that bill; he hadn't taken his suit to the cleaner's; he hadn't pruned that tree in the garden . . . And in the same vein it now occurred to him that he had an appointment in the city, that he would be very late if he walked, and that even the cab, which he immediately hailed, would not get him there on time . . .

The man waiting for him was a translator from a foreign country who for some days had been tracing the itineraries of a book set in the region and now wished to ask the author a few questions. The meeting place, a bar, was all that was left of a former movie house. The letters C I N E M A on the front had been roughly scraped off but were still visible. He was sitting there alone in the farthermost corner of the room, at first barely distinguishable from the photos of movie stars on the wall behind him. He might have been sitting there for an eternity, an old man, seemingly enlivened by waiting. He gave the writer a mischievous look, suggesting that he knew all about his afternoon, and greeted him as usual with a trope: "Is it not true that the abundance of fruit at the edge of the forest lures us into the middle, where there is nothing?"

The translator's questions were quickly answered (for, when asked about a word, the writer was able, after all, to explain what he had been up to). Once that was taken care of, the old man turned toward the dark lobby of the former movie house and launched into a speech, which came out as calmly and coherently as if he had composed it while waiting; and although he was foreign, not only to this city but also to Europe, his voice resounded in the bar as though he owned the place; for a moment, the fashionably dressed white-haired proprietress, who sat listening to the radio behind the long, curving brass counter, seemed to be his wife. Certain of his sentences were preceded—heralded, one might have said—by a long humming tone.

"You know, I myself was a writer for many years. If you see me so happy today, it's because I'm not one anymore. And now I'll tell you my reasons for feeling liberated. Listen, my friend. At the beginning of my writing days, I saw my inner world as a reliable sequence of images, which I had only to observe and describe one after another. But as time went on, the outlines lost their clarity, and in addition to looking into myself I found myself listening for something outside me. At the time I believed— and this belief was confirmed time and again—that a kind of Ur-text had been given to me in my innermost being, a text even more reliable than any interior image because the passage of time had no effect on it, because it was always there, identical with itself. I was convinced that if only I immersed myself in it in disregard of everything else, I would have no difficulty in transferring it to paper. In those days I thought of writing as a process of taking dictation, of translation, in which visible "copy" was replaced by a secret inner voice. But this dream fared no better than my other dreams; when instead of jotting down bits and pieces of it I tried to record it systematically, day after day, so as to produce a great Dream Book, it shrank and lost more of its meaning;

what couched in occasional fragments said everything said nothing when put forward as a systematic totality. My attempt to decipher a supposed Ur-text inside me and force it into a coherent whole struck me as original sin. That was the beginning of fear. More and more, I dreaded the moment when I would have to sit down and wait. I alone of all the writers known to me was afraid of writing, afraid day after day. And every night the same nightmare: I'm on a stage with a group of others, facing a big audience; all the others knew their lines, I was the only one who didn't. At the end I broke off in the middle of a sentence without feeling, without perception, without rhythm. That sentence hit me like a verdict: You are forbidden to write. Forever. Nothing more of your own. I remember how I went out into the hot sun that day and stood for hours under blossoming apple trees. I was as cold as any corpse, and yet I laughed as I thought of a great man's maxim: 'Just blow on your hands, then you'll be all right.' And after an interval of silence, I became what I am. Nothing more of your own! Don't cross the threshold. Stay in the forecourt. At last I can be a member of the cast, instead of having to act alone. Only as a member of the cast can I finally let go. Only as the translator—of a reliable text—can I enjoy the workings of my mind and feel intelligent. For now I know, as I did not before, that there is a solution for every problem. Yes, I still torture myself, but I no longer *suffer* torment and I no longer wait for my torment to cease so I can feel that I have a right to write. A translator has the certainty that he is needed. So I've got rid of my fear. And when I wake up in the morning, instead of dreading exile as I used to, I'm eager to get home to my translating. As a translator and nothing else, without secret reservations, I am entirely what I am; in my writing days I often felt like a traitor, but now, day after day, I feel that I'm true to myself. Translation brings me deep peace. And yet, my friend: I still experience the same marvels, but no longer in the role of an individual. The *mot juste* still gives me total satisfaction, and despite my age, my creeping gait becomes a running. I still feel the same urgency—but far from making me brood, it allows me to be refreshingly superficial. And by displaying your wound as attractively as possible, I conceal my own. And now that I've become a translator, I would gladly die at my desk."

Wishing to take a last look by himself at the city from which he had fled half a century before, the old man declined to let the writer accompany him back to his hotel. But the writer followed him in secret (as he often did with friends as well as strangers). Unobserved, he trailed close behind him across the squares, across the bridge, and then along the opposite bank. Although the translator, with his bobbing head and the hopping movements of a hare, seemed to be hurrying, his shadower, much as he had already slackened his pace, had to stop from time to time, for the old man not only zigzagged as though drunk but also paused every few steps to shift his bag with the translated manuscript to the other hand or set it down. It wasn't exactly a bag, but a wide, rectangular basket with a handle and a black leather lid that glittered like pitch in the light of every street lamp. What could be in it that's so heavy? And the writer saw it as the basket in which Miriam entrusted the infant Moses to the river Nile in the hope of saving him from the King's myrmidons. As far as the hotel door he had eyes only for the floating, bobbing basket in which lay hidden the infant Moses on his way to Pharaoh's daughter.

BACK HOME in his garden, he didn't know how he had got there. The details of his itinerary had escaped him, though he had walked steadily uphill, over stone steps and winding paths. The man on the dark riverbank, who had accompanied the river's murmuring on the saxophone, must have been a hallucination. Wasn't it another hallucination that he was in the garden now? Wasn't he in reality still sitting in the gin mill or lying dead somewhere, stabbed, shot, or run over by a car? He bent down and tried to make his first snowball of the year, but the flakes didn't stick together. It seemed to him in retrospect that in his hours away from his desk he had been locked in single combat—now at least it was no longer a hand-to-hand fight or a wrestling match. He paced the garden, circling every bush and tree, until his slowness became deliberation. There were lights in the house, he had left them on for his return. He sat down beside the door on the long wooden bench, which was something like the benches that peasant families sat on after the day's work. He was so warm that he unbuttoned his coat. He stretched out his legs and his heels felt the bumpy garden soil in its wintry quietness. Light fell on the fresh snow, which smelled more and more of fallen leaves and the rocky subsoil. The last campanula had been blasted by the frozen snow in its calyx; in a matter of hours, the luminous blue corolla had become shriveled and blackish-brown. The shell of the house next door, almost entirely overgrown with shrubbery because the owner had run out of money, stood there like a ruined temple on another continent. Then for a moment a workman opened his rule, shouts in a foreign language were heard, and the drum of the windlass, long still and choked with rust, began to turn. He remembered a day when during the lunch break the young apprentice had been lying on the flat roof, and he in his room, pounding away at the typewriter, had sent the apprentice his cosmic sound through the open window. Did he want a neighbor? Over this question he fell asleep and knew it: Receding voices, replaced by the One Voice, toneless and yet filling his cranial cavity, which told him his dreams. Told him about a book written by his predecessor, containing every single word he had written that day. The dream upset him for a moment, then soothed him. He gave himself a jolt and went into the house.

As usual he looked down involuntarily to see if some note or message had been dropped through the slit in the door, and as usual there was none. As usual he tangled his shoelaces while trying to untie them, and spent quite some time undoing the knots. And as usual, long after he had stepped into the entrance, his nameless cat stood motionless, staring at the door in expectation of someone else. Not being in the mood to talk to the animal, he fed it, and to make up for the withheld words cut the meat extra-small.

He switched off all the lights. Because of the snow and the reflection of the city in the clouds, it was light in all the rooms, a nocturnal light that made the objects in the rooms all the darker. In the kitchen, with his eyes on the luminous dial of the radio, he listened to the late news. Though it was midnight, the newscaster seemed as wide awake as if it were broad daylight. But in the middle of the news he was overpowered by emotion—what he was reading at the moment could not have accounted for it, it was due no doubt to something that had been on his mind the whole time. Almost voiceless, clearly on the brink of tears, once lapsing into a palpable silence, like a man clinging desperately to a window ledge from which he would fall with a scream. He barely made it to the weather report. After managing to squeeze out a "Good night," he was doubtless led away from the microphone. Had he just been fired? Had his girl left him? Had he been told of someone's death just before going on the air?

In one of the downstairs rooms from which he could see into another, the writer sat down in his night place, a kind of movie director's chair, from which he could see things at eye level. For a moment the light jacket hanging on the back of a chair—it had been there since last summer—made him feel the swimmer's wet eyelashes in the river wind. Why was it only when alone that he was able to participate fully? Why was it only after people had gone that he was able to take them into himself, the more deeply the farther away they went? Why did he conceive the most glowing image of those absent ones whom in his thoughts he saw as a couple? And why was it only with the dead that he truly lived? Why could only the dead become heroes in his mind? He laid one hand on his forehead and the other on his heart. He was sitting in a night train, which at that moment he actually heard rolling over the steel bridge down below with a sound like a sleigh in the snow. When the telephone rang in the entrance, he did not answer it. He wasn't expecting anyone to call and he didn't feel like opening his mouth again.

Not because he was tired but to stop himself from thinking any more, he steeled himself for the journey to his bedroom. While washing in the dark—sickened by the mere thought of seeing his face—he had the impression that someone was doing the same in the next room. He stopped washing. A book page was again being turned in the farthermost corner of the house. Again a chair was moved, again a cupboard was opened, and again the clothes hangers jangled together. Strange how in memory all sounds, even the sound of pottering and the squeaking of doors, merged into chords. Whatever was making that sound in the stairwell was too light-footed to be a human being.

As carefully as possible he took a glass and turned on the faucet very, very slowly so as to avoid the usual squeaking. Carrying the full glass in both hands, he started up the stairs; counting the steps made him slow down. Slow counting was better than brooding. It made him so light that the step he knew so well didn't give off the usual groan. Why had no one ever invented a god of slowness? Buoyed by his thought, he leapt over one step and a crash ran through the whole house as he landed.

He avoided going into his workroom and barely glanced at the table to see whether the white pile, to which a new page had been added each day since the summer, was still there. The nameless animal which had run up ahead of him lay there guarding the room, a hump on the carpet shaped like the hill the house was on. The writer opened the window beside the bed. This side of the house, opposite the garden, surmounted a sheer cliff. He saw himself falling; the impact, he thought, would be softened by the mass of pencil shavings that had accumulated down there over the years. (Often when falling asleep he had felt the tug of the abyss and resisted it by clutching the bedpost.) The treetops seemed rounded by the snow, and the sky had suddenly become starry clear. There, belted, stood the hunter Orion; at his feet the faint outline of the Hare, and a few handbreadths away, the Densely Sowed Ones, the Pleiades. The writer took a deep breath and was alone with the sky. The walking sticks of his various wanderings stood leaning against the wall in one corner of the room; the bronze hazel bark shimmered at eye level. What am I? Why am I not a bard? Or a Blind Lemon Jefferson? Who will tell me that I'm not nothing!

I started out as a storyteller. Carry on. Live and let live. Portray. Transmit. Continue to work the most ephemeral of materials, my breath; be its craftsman.

At last he would lie still and nothing else; yes, there was such a thing as rest. He thought of the next day and decided to tramp around the garden until his footprints were as dense as if a whole caravan had come through and until he had seen his first bird in flight. And he made another of his vows.

85]

If he didn't come to grief in his work, if he didn't lose his power of speech, he would give the chapel of the old people's home at the foot of the hill a bell which, instead of tinkling, would resound . . . And then he thought back on the afternoon and tried to visualize some part of it. Nothing came but the swaying branches in the opening between the curtains of the gin mill and the dog running around in a circle, baring its teeth as a boxer bares his mouthguard.

To himself he was a puzzle, a long-forgotten wonderment.

. . . 'tis all there, but I am nothing.

—GOETHE, *Torquato Tasso*